JOHNNY APPLESEED

JOHNNY APPLESEED

THE LEGEND AND THE TRUTH

By **Jane Yolen**

Illustrated by **Jim Burke**

HarperCollins*Publishers*

Library of Congress Cataloging-in-Publication Data
Yolen, Jane.
   Johnny Appleseed : the legend and the truth / by Jane Yolen ; illustrated by Jim Burke.— 1st ed.
     p.   cm.
   ISBN 978-0-06-059135-9 (trade bdg.) — ISBN 978-0-06-059136-6 (lib. bdg.)
   1. Appleseed, Johnny, 1774–1845—Juvenile literature. 2. Apple growers—United States—Biography—Juvenile literature. 3. Frontier and pioneer life—Middle West—Juvenile literature. I. Burke, Jim. II. Title.
SB63.C46Y65 2008
634'.11'092—dc22
2005017789
CIP
AC

Typography by Amelia May Anderson and Dana Fritts
1 2 3 4 5 6 7 8 9 10

First Edition

For Elizabeth Harding, who has seen me
through good times and bad, with loving thanks

—J.Y.

For my soul mate and apple of my eye—I love you, Suzanne.

—J.B.

Apple blossoms
Tap the sill,
Welcome baby
With a will,
Johnny, Johnny Appleseed.

THE HISTORY

Actually, it is a lovely autumn day
in Leominster, Massachusetts,
when the first Chapman son is born.
Outside the little rented cabin
the leaves are turning colors.
Apple trees on the nearby hills
groan with reddening fruit.
Suddenly, there's a cry from the cabin.
"A boy!" exclaims the midwife.
Nathaniel Chapman picks up his son
and shows the child to his wife,
lying on the wooden bed.
"We'll call him John," Chapman says.
Elizabeth Chapman smiles tiredly
and pats the arm of the four-year-old girl
who is standing by, watching.
"Lizzie, what do you want to call brother?"
"Johnny," the girl whispers.

 **THE FACT**

Recorded in the record book at Leominster meeting house:
"John Chapman Sun of Nathanael and Elizabeth Chapman.
Born at Leominster September ye 26th 1774."

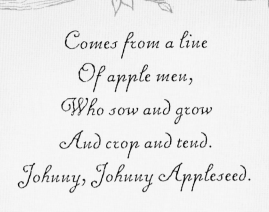

Comes from a line
Of apple men,
Who sow and grow
And crop and tend.
Johnny, Johnny Appleseed.

THE HISTORY

Chapman's great-great-great-great-granddad
came from England to Boston
and died in 1678, leaving his wife
"thirty good-bearing apple trees."
But Nathaniel is not much of a farmer.
He has no money to buy land.
Instead he rents a farm
from his wife's cousin.
To feed his growing family,
he plants turnips, corn, potatoes.
He does carpentry work.
And then Nathaniel goes off to war
as one of the minutemen,
under General George Washington,
fighting the British soldiers
in the American war for independence.

 ### THE FACT

Though Nathaniel enlists as a soldier and fights in the Battle
of Bunker Hill, his skill at carpentry soon ensures him a
place behind the lines, fixing wagons, constructing forts.

Eats only apples,
Drinks only juice,
Thinks as a boy
About apple use.
Johnny, Johnny Appleseed.

THE HISTORY

Elizabeth and the children
are left to fend for themselves,
stumbling through the seasons of war.
Relatives nearby help,
but the farm is a poor one.
Elizabeth is pregnant,
and sick with a lung disease.
Worried that they have no cow
to supply the children with fresh milk,
she writes to her husband on June 3
that cows "are very scarce and dear."
Exhausted from the birth
of her third child, a little boy,
she looks at her family, thinking
they will be safe with her parents.
Then she coughs and sighs.
They are the last sounds the children hear
from their mother.
A month later, the baby dies, too.

THE FACT

Elizabeth's letter was handed down in the family, as printed in
Johnny Appleseed Sourcebook (Fort Wayne, Indiana).

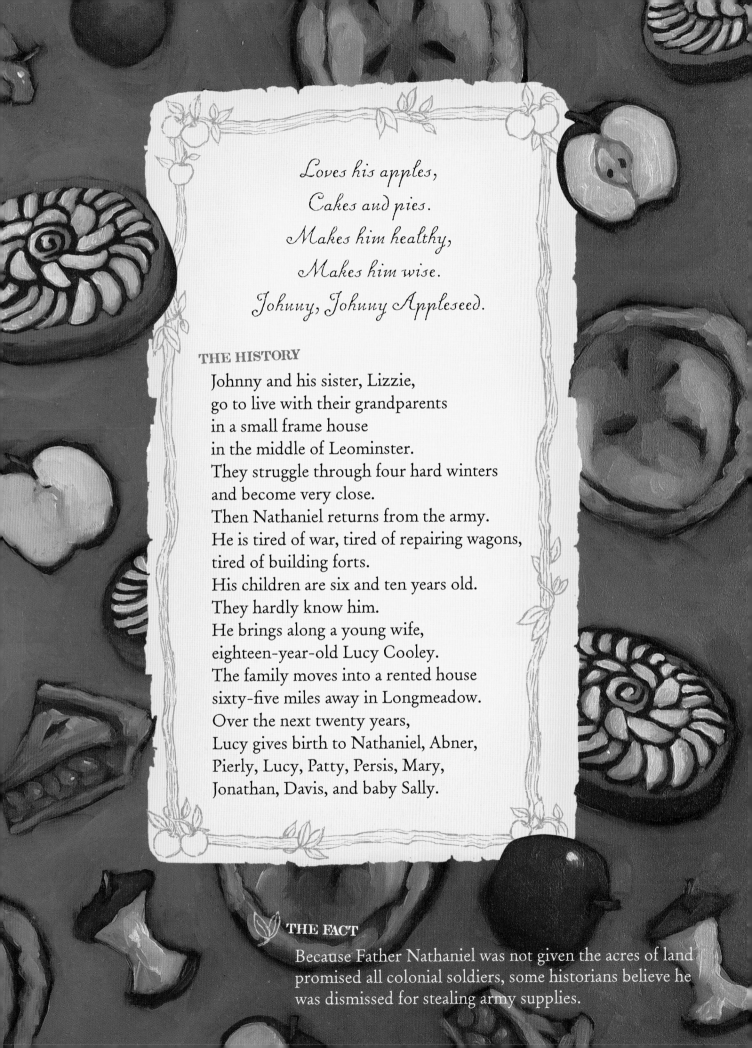

Loves his apples,
Cakes and pies.
Makes him healthy,
Makes him wise.
Johnny, Johnny Appleseed.

THE HISTORY

Johnny and his sister, Lizzie,
go to live with their grandparents
in a small frame house
in the middle of Leominster.
They struggle through four hard winters
and become very close.
Then Nathaniel returns from the army.
He is tired of war, tired of repairing wagons,
tired of building forts.
His children are six and ten years old.
They hardly know him.
He brings along a young wife,
eighteen-year-old Lucy Cooley.
The family moves into a rented house
sixty-five miles away in Longmeadow.
Over the next twenty years,
Lucy gives birth to Nathaniel, Abner,
Pierly, Lucy, Patty, Persis, Mary,
Jonathan, Davis, and baby Sally.

THE FACT

Because Father Nathaniel was not given the acres of land
promised all colonial soldiers, some historians believe he
was dismissed for stealing army supplies.

Learns to write,
Learns to read,
First word he pens
Is apple seed.
Johnny, Johnny Appleseed.

THE HISTORY

The Longmeadow house,
small and weather-beaten,
sits in a lush meadow, not far
from the winding Connecticut River
and deeply wooded hills.
Johnny and his sister and
their half brothers and half sisters
go to the Longmeadow school.
There Johnny learns to read
and write and cipher.
He learns penmanship.
Johnny takes to reading,
eagerly borrowing books.
Even more, he takes to the woods,
oak and maple, birch, beech, and pine.
There he watches the deer
drink from the river
and the red foxes leap
in and out of the high grass.

THE FACT

Two of the half brothers were deaf and as such would not
have gone to the local school but been taught at home.

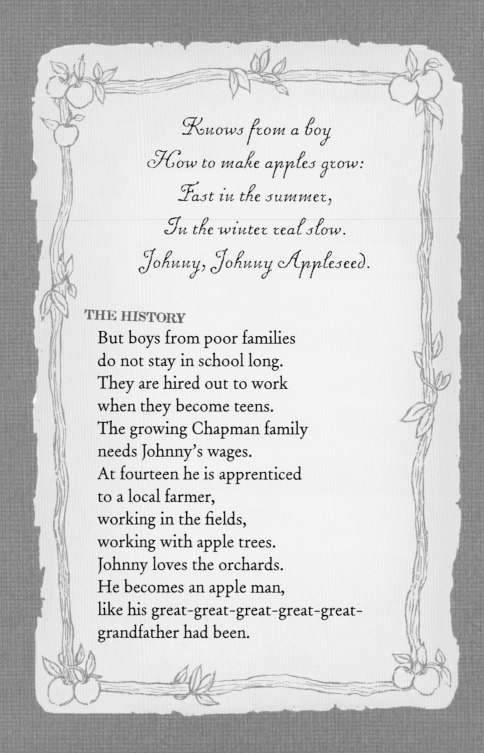

Knows from a boy
How to make apples grow:
Fast in the summer,
In the winter real slow.
Johnny, Johnny Appleseed.

THE HISTORY

But boys from poor families
do not stay in school long.
They are hired out to work
when they become teens.
The growing Chapman family
needs Johnny's wages.
At fourteen he is apprenticed
to a local farmer,
working in the fields,
working with apple trees.
Johnny loves the orchards.
He becomes an apple man,
like his great-great-great-great-great-
grandfather had been.

THE FACT

Apples are the perfect fruit. They can be eaten fresh or be dried, put
in pies or made into sauce, apple butter, cider, or vinegar, or even
fermented into an alcoholic drink. No other fruit is so useful.

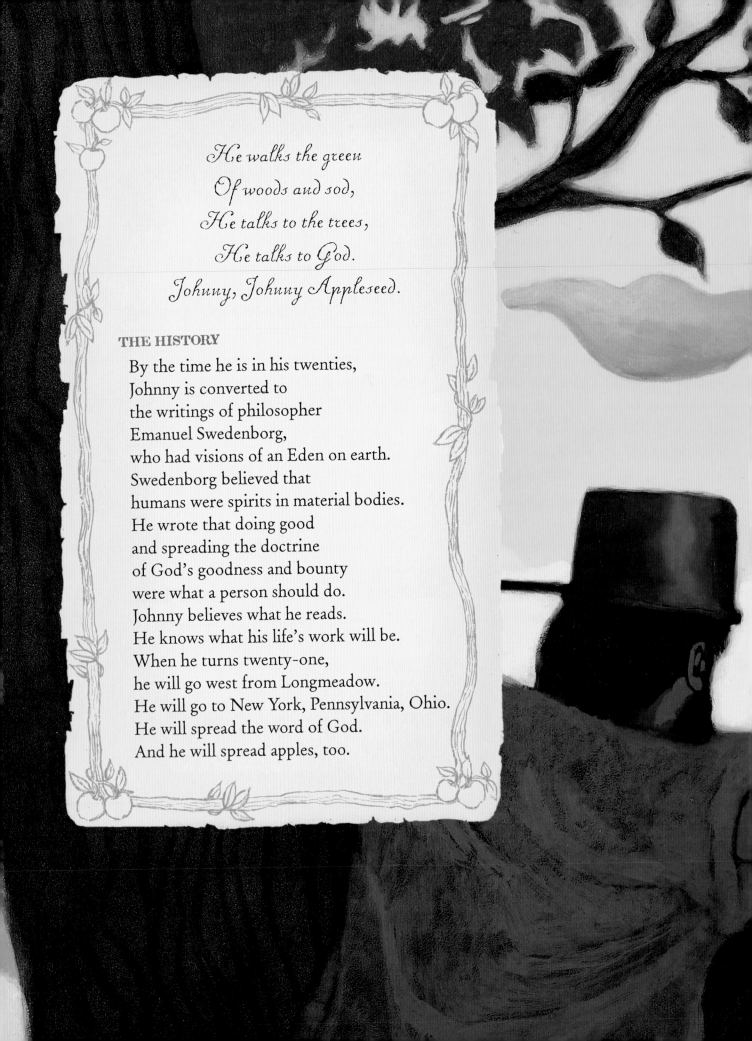

He walks the green
Of woods and sod,
He talks to the trees,
He talks to God.
Johnny, Johnny Appleseed.

THE HISTORY

By the time he is in his twenties,
Johnny is converted to
the writings of philosopher
Emanuel Swedenborg,
who had visions of an Eden on earth.
Swedenborg believed that
humans were spirits in material bodies.
He wrote that doing good
and spreading the doctrine
of God's goodness and bounty
were what a person should do.
Johnny believes what he reads.
He knows what his life's work will be.
When he turns twenty-one,
he will go west from Longmeadow.
He will go to New York, Pennsylvania, Ohio.
He will spread the word of God.
And he will spread apples, too.

THE FACT

The Swedenborgian Church of the New Jerusalem is not established until the early 1800s, but its missionaries are already traveling through America, and Johnny becomes one of them.

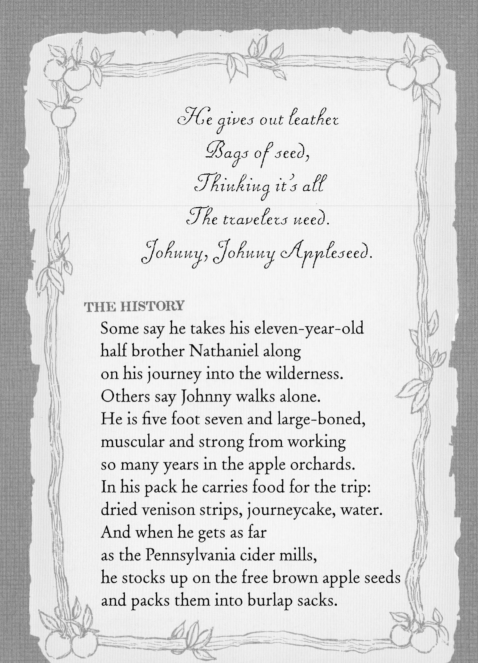

He gives out leather
Bags of seed,
Thinking it's all
The travelers need.
Johnny, Johnny Appleseed.

THE HISTORY

Some say he takes his eleven-year-old
half brother Nathaniel along
on his journey into the wilderness.
Others say Johnny walks alone.
He is five foot seven and large-boned,
muscular and strong from working
so many years in the apple orchards.
In his pack he carries food for the trip:
dried venison strips, journeycake, water.
And when he gets as far
as the Pennsylvania cider mills,
he stocks up on the free brown apple seeds
and packs them into burlap sacks.

THE FACT

Little is known about Johnny's first journey. There are tales, verses, songs, but those were all made up long after the fact. We know for certain that he left home in the 1790s, and by 1797 trading post ledgers near Franklin, Pennsylvania, record the names of John and Nathaniel Chapman.

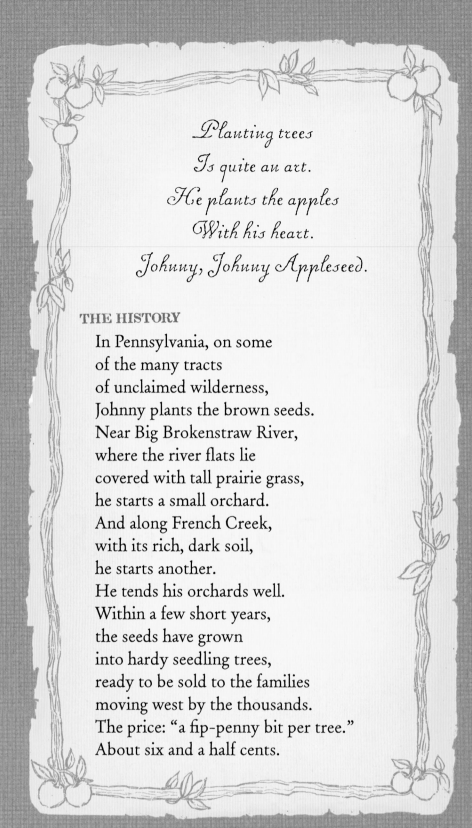

Planting trees
Is quite an art.
He plants the apples
With his heart.
Johnny, Johnny Appleseed.

THE HISTORY

In Pennsylvania, on some
of the many tracts
of unclaimed wilderness,
Johnny plants the brown seeds.
Near Big Brokenstraw River,
where the river flats lie
covered with tall prairie grass,
he starts a small orchard.
And along French Creek,
with its rich, dark soil,
he starts another.
He tends his orchards well.
Within a few short years,
the seeds have grown
into hardy seedling trees,
ready to be sold to the families
moving west by the thousands.
The price: "a fip-penny bit per tree."
About six and a half cents.

 THE FACT

Some land-grant companies insisted in their contracts that settlers
plant fifty apple trees on their land in the first year of owning it.

Tin-pot hat,
Ratty hair,
Clothes just rags,
Feet go bare.
Johnny, Johnny Appleseed.

THE HISTORY

Johnny is not a city man.
He loves the forests,
the meadows, the wilderness.
Often he sleeps outdoors.
His payment for trees
does not always come as money.
He is given cast-off clothes,
a bed for the night, a hearty dinner,
or sometimes food for the journey:
watermelons, cornmeal, salt pork.
He makes friends with the native people,
the Seneca and Munsee.
But by 1804, Pennsylvania
feels too settled, too crowded.
His half brother Nathaniel
has already gone on to Ohio.
Johnny borrows money from his family
to be repaid "in land or apple trees."
Then he goes west.

THE FACT

The IOU reads: "I promise to pay Nathaniel Chapman . . . the sum of one hundred dollars in land or apple trees." No one knows if this means his father or his brother lent him the money.

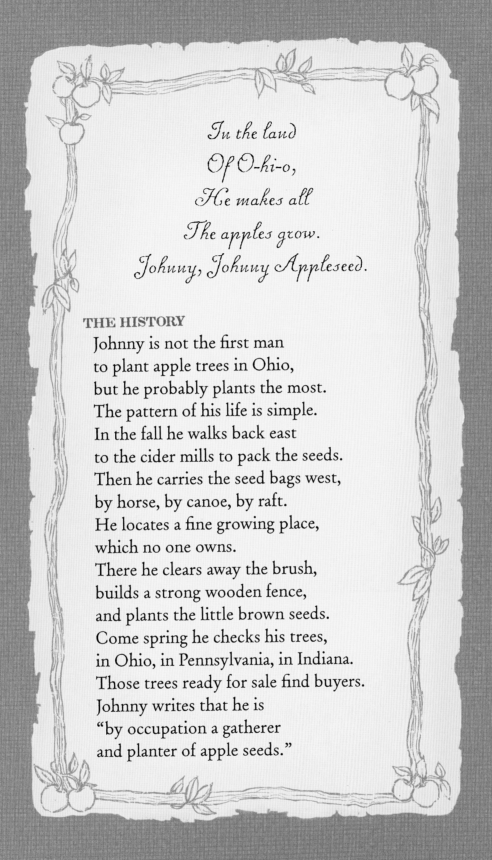

In the land
Of O-hi-o,
He makes all
The apples grow.
Johnny, Johnny Appleseed.

THE HISTORY

Johnny is not the first man
to plant apple trees in Ohio,
but he probably plants the most.
The pattern of his life is simple.
In the fall he walks back east
to the cider mills to pack the seeds.
Then he carries the seed bags west,
by horse, by canoe, by raft.
He locates a fine growing place,
which no one owns.
There he clears away the brush,
builds a strong wooden fence,
and plants the little brown seeds.
Come spring he checks his trees,
in Ohio, in Pennsylvania, in Indiana.
Those trees ready for sale find buyers.
Johnny writes that he is
"by occupation a gatherer
and planter of apple seeds."

 **THE FACT**

The first evidence John Chapman actually bought land
for orchards is recorded in 1809 in Mount Vernon, Ohio,
where he purchased two lots. By 1815, he owned 640 acres.

Walks barefoot
Through heavy snows,
Preaching Eden
As he goes.
Johnny, Johnny Appleseed.

THE HISTORY

There is no doubt Johnny is strange.
He is usually alone.
His clothes are castoffs.
His shirt is made from a coffee sack.
Often the shoes he wears are
secondhand sandals or boots.
He visits settlers' cabins
to preach the word of
the Church of the New Jerusalem
but then sleeps outside.
Whenever he goes to Ashland County,
he stays with his half sister
Persis Broom and her family,
bringing them gifts
of ribbons and buttons,
telling stories to the four girls.
And what stories he has to tell.

THE FACT

He loved to tell tales to children. Remembering Johnny Appleseed staying in his family's log cabin, Ohio native R. I. Curtis recalled, "He . . . would talk to me a great deal, telling me . . . of his adventures, and hair-breadth escapes. . . ."

Apple blossoms
Weep him down,
Appleseed
Of great renown.

THE HISTORY

Johnny looks like a poor old peddler,
but perhaps that is part of a plan,
for when he travels, he often
carries a great deal of money.
And then one day, going to Indiana
through the cold and rain,
he hears that cows have broken
through one of his orchard fences.
He walks fifteen miles to fix it.
Returning exhausted, he goes to bed,
sick with a fever
called "winter plague"—pneumonia.
He dies on March 18, 1845, in the middle of winter,
and is buried in Fort Wayne, Indiana, in a six-dollar coffin,
which costs two to three times an acre of land.
He is not quite seventy-one years old.
To everyone's surprise, he leaves much property.
He owns a gray horse,
fifteen thousand apple trees and two thousand seedlings
in orchards in Indiana and Ohio,
totaling eight hundred acres,
and two town lots in Mount Vernon.

THE FACT

Alas, bills and a greedy lawyer eat up most of Johnny's estate. After
everything is settled, his beloved half sister Persis receives only
$165.95. What he really leaves is a legend.

Everyone loves a legend.

And what a legend John Chapman left—of a crazy old man who had feet so hard a snake's fangs could not penetrate them, who put out his campfire rather than harm the mosquitoes that flew into it. Of a man who sowed apple seeds from Massachusetts all the way to California, who helped the Native Americans and white settlers with equal ease. It was said he wore a tin mush pot on his head and a coffee sack for a shirt and went shoeless even in the worst of snowstorms. Some of it was true; most of it was half true or totally made up.

Like most heroes of legend, Johnny Appleseed was thought to have had a magical birth, with apple blossoms tapping on the windowpane to welcome him, though he was actually born in the fall. Numerous stories told how he walked in the forests near his childhood home, with wild creatures flocking around him. And when he died, more stories circulated about apple blossoms falling on his grave, though it was still winter and several months until apple-blossom time.

Legends are like that. They take over the real life story. But John Chapman—Johnny Appleseed or Appleseed John, as he was alternately called—led a life that was in some ways even greater than the legends. He really did change the landscape of the country, planting great apple orchards and selling them to thousands of westward travelers till all of America was apple land, from sea to shining sea.

—J.Y.